MEMORY GAMES

A SHORT STORY

INCLUDED IN 'YOUR MOTHER'S NIGHTMARES', A
COLLECTION OF SIX TROUBLING TALES

ANITHA KRISHNAN

DREAM PEDLAR BOOKS

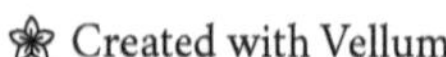 Created with Vellum

For Dhruv,
the greatest miracle in my life.
Thank you for showing me that perfection is never the goal.
Consciousness is. That has made all the difference.

~

ABOUT THIS BOOK

Memory Games

On the morning after his seventh birthday, Skyla gives her son a gift without his knowledge. Also, without his consent.

She has all his painful memories excised from his brain.

She considers it the best gift of all. The memory of a perfect childhood.

But no one could possibly gift something that simply does not exist. At least, not without unfortunate consequences.

Memory Games secured an Honourable Mention in the L. Ron Hubbard Writers of the Future Contest (July—September 2023).

BEFORE WE BEGIN

Dear Reader,

Motherhood, or even parenting in general, is one of those life experiences that are almost universal yet remarkably unique to each one of us.

Everyone's parenting journey is vastly different. What works for one parent/family may simply not work for another.

My own journey has been a mix of unimaginable joys and unbelievable anxieties and everything else in between these two extremes.

During those dark moments, I turned to writing as a salve. I couldn't bring myself to speak aloud the fears I had for my child. Already wracked with anxiety and a deep sense of wrongness for even having those fears in the first place, I was terrified that putting them in written or spoken form—by journalling or talking about them to someone—might just make them come true.

Instead, I couched them in the guise of speculative fiction to render them more palatable, more surmountable, and as a reminder that in those moments my fears were exactly that—fiction!

It's for this very reason that I crafted the short story collection, *Your Mother's Nightmares*, a few months ago. *Memory Games* is a short story from that six-tale collection.

If you're a parent, my hope is that in these pages, you too will find the words for the darkness you already know so intimately and grapple with every single day, and emerge into the light on the other side, feeling seen and sane and safe in the knowledge that you are doing the best you can and that is more than enough.

~ Anitha Krishnan
Burlington, Ontario,
Tuesday, 18 June 2024

MEMORY GAMES

1
———

Skyla's heart leapt into her throat as the technician gently lifted Rowen's head with gloved hands and draped what appeared like a black swim cap over it. Thin black wires emerged from the base of the cap and fed into a machine, no bigger than a shoe box, placed on a low side-table beside the bed.

A skull-and-crossbones image on the contraption would have been apt, Skyla thought, chewing on her fingernails nervously.

"Are you certain this will work?" she asked for the umpteenth time that morning. It was all she could think of.

The technician smiled and nodded without looking up from her work, which at this point entailed tugging the skullcap evenly from all sides and ensuring it covered the child's head completely.

"No side effects?"

"None at all," the technician replied, again without looking up.

Skyla chewed her fingernails and tried to calm herself

down. Other than the fact that she knew what was about to happen, there was nothing in this room that appeared threatening to her or her seven-year-old boy in any way whatsoever.

Rowen lay fast asleep in a soft bed with a white sheet and pillow covers with a printed design of blue waves and colourful little sailboats all over. A duvet with a matching cover was pulled up to his chin. Even in this anaesthetic stupor, he slept with his mouth innocently open and his favourite Squishmallow, Rutabaga the caterpillar, tucked under the duvet beside him.

The bed was up against a pastel blue wall on which fluffy white clouds and V-shaped gulls had been painted. A piece of sky in the basement.

Skyla caught an occasional whiff of fresh laundry, a breezy, light-hearted scent, but she couldn't tell if it was her imagination reacting to the sight of the wall décor or the effect of a subtle fragrance dispenser tucked out of sight.

The theme of blue skies and white clouds continued on all the walls. Against one wall beside the bed was a neat arrangement of shelves in white and pastel shades, bearing books and an assortment of toys. Against another was a large white table and bright yellow swivel chair set up under a board to which were pinned what appeared to be family photographs with children laughing, grown-ups beaming, sun shining, and grass gleaming.

It all made the room appear as if it had sprung into existence straight from an IKEA catalogue. Fresh and charming. Exactly what a child's room was supposed to look like.

They were in one of the basement rooms of what had

turned out to be a very well looked after Georgian house. Skyla had lured her newly seven-year-old to the place citing the necessity of annual medical check-ups.

"Why aren't we going to Dr. Kamal then? We always go there," Rowen had asked, much to Skyla's chagrin. Her boy was growing up too fast. He knew too much. He remembered too much.

She made some excuse about Dr. Kamal being away on vacation and that had seemed to satisfy Rowen, who promptly ran into the gardens of the house to inspect the rows of tulips that were in full bloom.

She would have to erase his memory of this conversation too; she couldn't afford to have him inquiring Dr. Kamal about a vacation that had never taken place.

A path through the garden had led them around to the back of the house where a steep flight of stairs and then a bright red door with a mischievous-looking brass pixie on the knocker granted them access to the room they were now in.

Skyla had been pleasantly surprised at how pleasing and welcoming the room was, while Rowen had delightedly run straight to the shelves of books and toys. She had never managed to achieve that effect in Rowen's own bedroom back at home, so it gave her some consolation that the procedure was set to be conducted in a room like this, although a pang of grief plucked at her heart that her child would leave this place holding no memory of it.

A large screen took up the entire wall opposite the bed. It flickered into life as the technician, now having discarded her gloves, pressed a button on a flat handheld device smaller than her palm, pointing it at the screen.

The technician was a short, plump woman with silver hair

that sprung up in thick but obedient curls around her kind face. Curious brown eyes peered from behind tortoiseshell glasses with chains. She was smartly dressed in a pastel pink skirt suit but she smelt of muffins and icing, of cookies and chocolate.

Skyla decided to call her Mrs. M in her mind. A codename. Like in the James Bond stories. There was a decidedly furtive air to it all. Besides, M could also stand for Memories. That made it easier to remember.

Moreover, Mrs. M had declined to reveal her name nor had she asked Skyla for her or her child's names. The less they knew about each other, the less likely they'd compromise each other, Mrs. M had insisted, especially since the procedure was only in its nascence.

"You won't believe the number of times people swear they can weather the risks and side-effects, but the instant trouble comes knocking on their door, they come looking for me to blame," Mrs. M had explained to Skyla on her first visit about a month ago.

Yet, the technician had insisted that there would be no side effects to what they were about to attempt. Skyla felt the need to verify again, now that the moment of reckoning had arrived what with Rowen lying with that contraption on his head at one end of the room and on the other end, fractal images curling and unfurling, expanding and shrinking in an eerie psychedelic dance on the screen.

"But you said there won't be any side effects?" Skyla asked, narrowing her eyes. "Then why would people come looking to blame you?"

The old lady looked up at Skyla with understanding eyes. "It is terrifying to face up to what you've desired for so long, isn't it? Because what if it doesn't solve the problems you had hoped it would?"

Tears moistened Skyla's eyes and she let them spill. Mrs. M held out a box of tissues from which Skyla pulled out one and dabbed at her eyes.

"It is," she sniffled. "What if it messes up his mind in some unexpected way?"

Mrs. M waited for a few moments before replying, "It's quite like forgetting. He won't remember what he doesn't know he once knew." She paused, as if allowing Skyla to untangle and correctly interpret that particular sequence of words. "You cannot miss what you don't know you had."

That, Skyla understood very well.

2

Fatherless since the age of three, Skyla had grown up with her mother and grandparents. Life had been just perfect until three years later she had stumbled upon a photograph of her father carrying Skyla in one arm, his other arm wrapped around his wife, the three of them laughing into the camera at some joke the photographer had said, wide, open-hearted grins lighting up their faces. That photograph in all its sepia-tone glory had caused her world to burst open in a way she had never known before. She began to remember things it was impossible to remember.

She could see clearly in her mind's eye how he stayed up all night holding her when she refused to sleep in her cot, how he'd throw her high up in the air and catch her every single time, laughing and giggling, how he could spend an entire afternoon pushing her on the swing without complaint, how he made eating all her veggies one of the most delightful parts of mealtime.

But those memories brought along with them the raw,

heart-rending grief of what she'd never have again: life experiences with her father.

Ever since, being fatherless became a significant part of her identity, her only identity, and her excuse for getting into trouble and sabotaging her own life and future, until John had come along and whisked her off her feet. Then he too went and died before Rowen was born, and if that wasn't a sign from the Universe, what else could be?

She had to see to it that Rowen did not suffer the same fate she had. She couldn't let him become a victim of his own memories.

3

———

When the tears stopped and Skyla found she could speak once more without hiccuping for breath, she nodded and said, "OK, let's do this."

Mrs. M taught her how to work the remote. Right arrow for fast-forward. Left arrow for rewind. A play/pause button in the centre. And a red round button at the bottom for delete.

The system would not prompt for a confirmation, Mrs. M warned. The instant Skyla pressed the Delete button, the memory would begin to get erased until she pressed the button again.

"And there is no way to retrieve any of the deleted memories?" Skyla asked.

Mrs. M opened her mouth as if to say something, then peered at Skyla through her tortoiseshell glasses on which the reflections of the fractal images on the screen danced. It was almost cartoon-like and Skyla was gripped with a sudden urge to laugh at the wild absurdity of it all.

"There is a reason you want those memories gone, isn't it?" Mrs. M said at last.

Skyla simply nodded, keeping her lips pursed, afraid of what strange sound might spill out of her mouth if she let it. A strangled laugh. A cry of uncertainty. A sob. A scream, perhaps?

"Then let's get on with it, shall we?" Mrs. M said. She went up to the desk and chair beside the screen and rolled the yellow swivel chair towards Skyla, gesturing to her to sit on it.

"You will be at it for a few hours," Mrs. M said mysteriously as Skyla sank into the soft chair, holding the remote gingerly in her hand, afraid she'd press the wrong button accidentally.

"Good luck," Mrs. M said, then left the room, closing the door quietly behind her.

Skyla pulled herself closer to the bed and looked at Rowen for a few moments. Why hadn't anyone ever told her how hard life could be?

Her mother and grandparents had always insisted that given time and trust, she'd be able to face any situation and overcome any challenge that life threw her way. For a while she had believed that, but then she lost John and found out that there were always exceptions to the rule.

The sight of Rowen's sleeping face steeled her resolve. Now this was a difficult task she'd see through, she told herself and set to work.

4

———————

A heart beats inside a womb. Liquid darkness flows all around it. Voices in the distance, from somewhere outside.

A tiny fist reaches out, touches the wall.

Squeals of delight sound on the other side. Something glows. Someone calls out in a voice so loving and tender.

What lies outside? The infant wants to know. He is eager to slip out and see. He can't help it. He has to push his way through, head first.

The screams are deafening. Muffled still, but louder than ever before. He can hear the startling pain in those wails. Is something wrong?

Push, push, he hears someone say, and he feels the walls of his home pushing against his feet, squeezing him further and further through the birth canal.

And then he is out.

A shock of cold hits him all over, and now it is his turn to open his mouth and draw breath and let out a cry.

That seems to please everyone. There are tears and

laughter, and now he is being placed on something soft and warm, on someone safe, someone who loves him so much, he can already tell. Someone who wraps his arms around him and coos into his ears and kisses him all over and makes him feel warm and safe all over again.

5

___

kyla hit the pause button. She needed a moment, just a moment.

This was ridiculous. Even though Mrs. M had explained to her exactly what it is she'd see on the screen, she hadn't expected it to be like this. She hadn't been prepared to see the past unfold from her child's mind. Not from the instant he had come into existence inside her womb.

Did people really have memories of that time? How is it that you could spend an entire lifetime designating each moment to memory, to history, only to have very little recollection of any of it afterwards? Where did all those memories disappear to?

But they didn't really disappear, did they? Rowen's memories were right here, being extracted from some unknown part of his brain by that skull-cap on his head and fed into the shoebox machine on the other side of the bed from where they were projected onto the screen like a movie.

A video recording of childhood, except it was all from Rowen's perspective. And she could feel everything he had felt at that point in time. All his fears and his joys, his curiosity about this new world he had found himself in, and his frustration at not being able to make sense of it all right away.

It was as though she had become him, in reliving his memories and feeling all his feelings.

The initial shock wore off and Skyla continued her journey through Rowen's memories, more intrigued and less intimidated now.

There were many, many happy memories, many more than she had believed. Good! There'd be less to wipe out, she thought and that gave her some relief.

Every time she saw her smiling face through Rowen's eyes as she bent down to pick him up for a cuddle, pride surged through her heart. She had been a good mom, she really had tried very hard.

There she was, the first person he saw when he opened his eyes after a daytime nap.

There she was again, squatting, arms outstretched, face lit with a wide smile, as he went down a little slide and slid off and straight into her waiting arms.

There she was again, cleaning a bruise on his knee, putting a bandaid on it and kissing it, promising him it would heal in a jiffy. There had been a time when her assurances were all he needed to bounce back from pain and disappointment, when her word had been enough to restore him to a place of safety.

And then her first mistake.

At the age of two.

Skyla could feel Rowen's terror grip her entire body as she saw her own face bearing down on her on the screen, red with anger, her mouth spitting harsh words at her toddler who had somehow managed to topple a large basket full of thermocol balls on to the floor and had been jumping up and down happily, chasing those slippery balls, scooping them in his little hands and throwing them up, calling out, "Se-no, Se-no," able to manage only a childlike warped pronunciation of 'snow'.

Rowen's fear and shame flooded her entire body as he sat, in his memory, in a corner, tears streaming down his cheeks and snot filling his nose, little hands clamped over his ears, watching his mother hoover up all the little balls that had given him so much delight now disappear into that loud, roaring machine, which was still no match for how loud and angry his mother's bellows were as she continued to curse his very existence and his innate ability to make a mess around him wherever he went.

6

———

*S*kyla hit the pause button again, and only when the video on the screen froze and the sound was cut off, did she hear the whimpers that wracked her body alternating with her own loud, uncontrollable wails filling the room.

She whipped her head around, worried the commotion may have awoken Rowen. He remained asleep, completely oblivious to the goings-on around him. His face glowed in the light from the paused video on the screen in that pale, ghostly way that skin shines under moonlight.

Was he dreaming? Or was he safe in the depths of some dreamless sleep, a realm of the subconscious she had long lost access to ever since John had died and Rowen was born and her mind had once again opened up to the terrifying inevitabilities of loss and grief, of pain and sorrow?

Skyla looked back at the screen where her own angry face from five years ago glared down at her, eyes grown too large to be held back in their sockets anymore, teeth bared and lips curled in a snarl as her mouth was frozen in mid-expletive, a face twisted and contorted in anger.

And for the first time she could reach out and touch the fear that hovered just beneath her skin. And when she touched it, she could go even further and feel the pain and grief lurking beneath it all.

In that moment, as Skyla sat in a yellow swivel chair in the basement of a beautiful Georgian house, trusting the contraptions set up by an unknown Mrs. M to weed out memories of bad experiences from her child's mind and psyche, she saw her world expand.

The spirit that throbbed deep inside her being swelled and ballooned and grew larger and larger, a bubble widening beyond the walls of this room, past the boundaries of this house, breaking every visible and invisible barrier that stood between her and the rest of the world.

And in doing so, her spirit encompassed the hurt and the pain of every child that had ever been birthed and brought into existence in this world, and throbbed with the grief of every mother and father that had ever had to struggle with the impossible responsibility of raising a child well.

In the inexplicable vastness of her heart she could now hold the pain of every form of life that had once been a helpless infant or a vulnerable seedling, that had ever been wronged, and alongside she could also hold deep compassion for everyone that had caused pain, knowingly or unknowingly, monsters not even of their own making.

Because, Skyla was finally beginning to see that her pain was no different than that of the world, the way she hurt her child and the way she was hurting inside were just as valid as the terror and fear the little one felt in his veins, just as valid and honest and true as the confusion she herself must have felt when at the receiving end of rebuke and reprimand, no matter how well-intentioned, from her own mother or her grandparents, even from her teachers or that random stranger on the road who likely believed he knew much more about raising a child than every other parent on earth put together.

And if that were true, then no sin in this world was unpardonable because if no one was of their own making alone, but a product of every external influence and life experience that had begun shaping them even before they were born, that was shaping them even now, then no person's sin, or even virtue, was of their own making.

Something released itself from deep within Skyla's gut, something like an absolutely rigid knot of guilt that had weighed down her soul to inaccessible depths came bubbling up from her belly to her throat and slipped out with the sigh that escaped from her lips. Whatever it was, drifted away, like the white tufty clouds that dotted the blue sky imagery on the walls around her.

She forced herself to look into the angry face that scowled at her from the screen. "It's OK," she whispered to her red raging face on the screen. Her past-self from five years ago continued to stare at her disbelievingly, for it could never be OK that she had ever inflicted such torment on her child, could it?

"It's OK," Skyla whispered again, "you're only human. Besides, we're fixing it now, aren't we?"

Perhaps it was her imagination, or perhaps it was her change in perspective, but the image on the screen began to soften. The anger in that frozen face seemed to dissolve and Skyla could clearly see the grief and fear that lurked beneath it all.

The grief of losing John. The fear of raising a child as a

single mother. The worry of not being able to do him justice. The constant, nagging fear that she was always falling short. The harsh critical voice inside her mind that insisted she had already screwed up Rowen's life in every which way possible.

Because didn't all the parenting experts insist that every behavioural problem you exhibited now, every fear and anxiety that held you back, had their roots in your early upbringing?

The first seven years of our lives were all that mattered, and then we spend the rest of our lives undoing what was done to us in those first seven years. Who had said that? Was it Steiner? Or was it Montessori?

Whoever it was, their words were now being regurgitated by every parenting expert, and goodness, how many of them had proliferated in this world in just the past decade?

It was as if everywhere she turned, someone stood with a book or a podcast or a video or a word of advice, intent on showing her just how badly she was screwing up every single moment as a parent, as a mother, as a human being.

She too was not a mother of her own making. She too was heavily under the influence of all these external stimuli, whether she resisted or succumbed to them, it didn't matter. She was under their influence all the same, and it shaped and twisted her in ways she could barely ever control.

"It's OK," she whispered to Skyla-on-the-screen again.

Then she rewound the video to the instant where her angry tirade had begun, and pressed the Delete button.

7

———

*R*owen was seventeen years old when a girl first broke his heart.

"What did I do wrong?" he kept asking his mother over and over again, and when she had no satisfactory answers to give him, he disappeared into the music of Pink Floyd and Metallica that poured through his headphones into his ears, drowning out all voices from outside and from inside his own head.

Skyla pottered about in Rowen's room on days like these. Gone were the nightlights shaped like a star and a crescent moon. Gone were the growth mindset posters she had put up on the walls for encouragement and motivation. Gone were the baskets full of LEGO bricks and pieces that had, at one point in time, taken up a permanent spot besides Rowen's bed.

The walls were now covered in posters featuring the album covers of Pink Floyd and other bands the names of which weren't familiar. A large triangle splitting a single beam of light into a rainbow of colours. Another featuring a quartet wearing more metal than clothes, glaring out of the poster with kohl-lined eyes in a way that could have been threatening or enticing, it was always hard to tell.

The table and chair had grown larger with Rowen, as had the bed, but they had also grown tidier over the years. Gone was the scent of baby shampoo; the room now had an unusually thick scent of deodorant mingled with sweat.

Skyla threw the curtains and windows open. She had always loved the fact that Rowen's room had large windows on both the southern and western sides. Light from the late afternoon sun flooded into the room, riding on a cool, gentle breeze carrying birdsong and the perfume of spring nascence.

Rowen didn't seem to mind her presence and occasionally stepped out of his heartbroken stupor to join in her attempts at tidying up. For that, she was grateful.

She had heard horror stories of how teenagers hated having their parents in their space. Ever since Rowen was a toddler, she had been dreading that eventuality, and even when it never came she couldn't help worry that some day it would happen and her carefully constructed life would collapse without warning all around her.

"It hurts so much, you know," Rowen said, watching leaf-shadow dance on the wall behind his bed. "I never knew anything could hurt so much."

Skyla could have told him then, recounted all the times she had hurt him with a sharp rebuke or a nasty glare. She could have told him about all the times she had hurt him, sometimes even relishing in the sense of power and control it used to give her, and his surprising ability to bounce back and forgive her and love her unconditionally as if nothing untoward had transpired in the first place.

But those memories were gone for him, etched stronger in

her mind though, and after his seventh birthday she had been nothing but the perfect Zen mother.

Understanding when he had glued his T-shirts together. Unflappable when he had come home from the playground with a bloody nose. Calm when she had been called to the emergency room where the school had had to send him when he had ended with a broken ankle after a rather energetic game of basketball.

Serene and tranquil as she was now, watching him nurse a broken heart, even as her own heart cried inside at the sight of her son's pain.

"This is the most difficult phase," she said, quelling the urge to convince him that this too shall pass, that other girls will waltz in and out of his life for no fault of his, and that life will continue to throw curveballs his way. He was a strong man now, she wanted to remind him, not burdened by any childhood trauma that would trip him up in life. She had ensured that at least.

He nodded, then resumed listening to the music he had paused to engage in that brief snippet of conversation. His hair fell over his eyes and he pushed it away. He had never liked that, any barrier between him and the world and all that it had to offer, not even when he was a child.

____

8

Rowen's psychiatrist looked uncannily like Mrs. M, if Mrs. M hadn't aged a day in the past seventeen years. It was a sign, Skyla thought.

Only, the psychiatrist called herself Dr. Rodriguez but that didn't change the fact that she was a short, plump woman with a curly silver bob and brown eyes framed in tortoiseshell glasses. She was dressed in a dark skirt suit, like a senior executive of a Fortune 500 company, but her perfume had the impossible aroma of chocolate and cookies.

Her office wasn't decked out like a child's bedroom but was all dark wood furniture with plush sofas and cozy bookshelves against a backdrop of forest green walls. Pot lights lit up the room in a warm, comfortable glow.

At Skyla's insistence, Rowen had started seeing Dr. Rodriguez a few months ago, shortly after he had turned twenty-four. After that first heartbreak seven years earlier, Skyla saw her boy grow addicted to getting high on weed, drop out of university and backpack around the world, and fall in and out of love faster than day could turn into night and back into day. It was almost as if he had developed an aversion to everything that was good and stable and secure in life.

A few sessions in, Dr. Rodriguez had wanted to meet Rowen along with Skyla, if she was willing and able, to better understand his childhood. Skyla had been terrified at first when her son had texted her about his psychiatrist's request, but she had promptly replied "Yes" with conviction.

It must be Mrs. M, Skyla thought, sitting across the desk from the kind, old lady. Why else would the psychiatrist want to meet her? Rowen was an adult now, old enough to attend therapy on his own without a parent accompanying him.

"Have we met before?" Skyla ventured, worried that Dr. Rodriguez would deny knowing her.

But the psychiatrist smiled kindly and said, "Perhaps our paths crossed a long time ago. I've been in this line of work for a very long time now."

Hope bloomed in Skyla's heart. Perhaps she could confide in the psychiatrist, tell her the truth, after all.

She turned to look at Rowen who had made himself comfortable on a wide two-seater sofa in the centre of the room. Legs in socks dangling over one arm of the sofa, he lay supine, taking up the entire length. He had one arm over his forehead, another over his belly. He appeared relaxed in a way Skyla hadn't seen him in a long, long time.

"Does he confide in you? About what ails him?" Skyla asked, turning back to face Dr. Rodriguez.

"Rowen is looking for the perfect woman," Dr. Rodriguez said, looking at Rowen in a manner of contemplation. "He seeks a perfect relationship, and I daresay you are to blame for that."

Skyla shrank back at those words in a frisson of anger. Unfazed, Dr. Rodriguez turned to look at her and smiled. "I don't mean that in an accusatory way. I'm sure you know we all recreate in our adult life the patterns we experienced in childhood, especially with our primary caregivers."

"I know," Skyla said, "which is why I strove to be a perfect mother to Rowen. Maybe I tried too hard, but his father died before he was even born, you know that? I took great care to ensure that home remained a safe and comforting place for Rowen. I wanted him to trust he could always count on me, that no matter what life threw at him, he always had a safety net in me, in home. Shouldn't that have made him a strong man? Capable of weathering all the ups and downs of life? That is what all the parenting experts said. Back then, at least!"

"I understand," Dr. Rodriguez said. "Rowen says he's had a very happy childhood, that he can't recall a single unpleasant experience with you. But, you see, sometimes it's what we don't know about ourselves that haunts us. The ghosts of our forgotten selves."

Skyla was shocked. "You know, don't you?" she gasped.

"Know what?"

"About his memories," Skyla whispered, afraid of what she'd hear next.

The doctor nodded. "I know he cannot access them, not his early ones anyway. We have tried hypnosis. It didn't work." She peered into Skyla's eyes, almost accusingly, and asked, "Are we looking for something that no longer exists?"

Skyla barely managed to croak out the words through the fear that seemed to be strangling her. "I thought it was for the best."

9

"Our brains do not develop fully until we are in our mid-to-late-twenties," Dr. Rodriguez said, as she slipped something like a black swim cap over the top of Rowen's head.

He was asleep on the couch, heavily sedated.

Dr. Rodriguez fetched a blanket, which Skyla draped over Rowen and tucked under his chin. An eerie sense of déjà vu filled her being.

"Are you saying what was done can be undone?" Skyla asked hopefully, without turning to look back at Dr. Rodriguez.

"We can always try," the doctor said.

Skyla spun around to face the doctor. "And what side-effects will it have this time?"

"I shall repeat what I said to you seventeen years ago, and I will also tell you something I've learnt since."

Skyla held her breath. This was as close a confirmation she'd ever get that Dr. Rodriguez and Mrs. M were one and the same person.

"It is true," the doctor was saying, "you cannot miss what you don't know you once had. But perfection is never a worthy objective to pursue. The more acceptance we have towards our mistakes and failures, the better off we'll be in the long run."

Dr. Rodriguez/Mrs. M/Fairy Godmother pressed a concealed button on the side of the sofa by Rowen's head. A white screen rolled down from a recess in the ceiling in front of a bookshelf-lined wall.

Clearly, Dr. Rodriguez/Mrs. M had kept up with the latest technology, and that instilled some confidence in Skyla, a sliver of hope that she could set things right, notwithstanding the doctor's advice to be more tolerant towards her deeds and misdeeds, she realized wryly.

The doctor pressed a remote in Skyla's hand. Right arrow for fast-forward. Left arrow for rewind. A play/pause button in the centre. And a green round button at the bottom for Retrieve.

The system would not prompt for a confirmation, the doctor warned. The instant Skyla pressed the Retrieve button, the memory would begin to be implanted back into Rowen's brain until she pressed the button again.

"I thought you said the memories were deleted forever," Skyla said.

"No," the doctor said, pressing her lips to hide a grin. "You asked me if there was no way to retrieve any of the deleted memories. And I didn't quite give you an answer."

10

____

"Lilly poured thermocol balls all over the kitchen the other day, you know?" Rowen said to Skyla one evening just as she was about to leave for home.

She had spent the entire day caring for her two-year-old granddaughter while Rowen, now thirty-one years old, attended medical school, training to become a brain surgeon, and Kiara, his wife of five years, ran a flourishing publishing business out of her downtown office.

One last month of summer, and then Lilly would begin to attend a popular daycare in the neighbourhood. Skyla's services as a daytime caregiver would no longer be required, except in the case of illnesses and emergencies.

"You've been a tremendous help," her daughter-in-law had said very graciously, "and we can never thank you enough for all that you've done. It would do Lilly some good to spend more time around children her age now. Lilly loves you. Rowen and I do too."

Skyla had understood, yet she couldn't help feel a little sad.

It was as though her nest was about to become empty once more.

"She loves thermocol balls, yes," she replied absent-mindedly to Rowen as she stepped out of his home into the bright summer evening.

The sky was a delicious blue. White tufty clouds drifted past like sailboats. A gentle breeze tousled the tops of the maples that arched over the quiet and pretty suburban street Rowen and his family lived on.

Skyla slipped her sunglasses over her eyes, then turned to him and said, "You did too, when you were her age, you know?"

"Really?" Rowen scratched his days-old beard. His eyes were bloodshot from lack of sleep. "I bet that drove you mad."

Skyla laughed. "Very!"

But the very next instant, tears sprung into her eyes and she was glad for the sunglasses that hid her grief from Rowen. "It was the first time I yelled at you."

Her voice faltered, and once the words started to come out, she couldn't stop them. "There was thermocol everywhere, and it was just the two of us, just me all alone, really, trying to look after you and worried that you didn't have a father in your life. A boy needs his father, you know? And I knew you'd be needing your snack and a nap real soon, but I hadn't slept well in days, and the sight of all those … all those little weightless balls everywhere, it … it just drove me mad, having to add yet another task to my endless to-do list. I am so sorry, Rowen, I am so sorry."

The tears streamed down her cheeks, and Rowen was startled. "It's alright, Mom. I don't even remember you ever screaming at me. But even if you did, I get it. I totally get it."

Rowen pulled Skyla into a hug and said, "Kiara and I would have hardly stayed sane had it not been for you doing the bulk of the work when it came to Lilly. And you had no one, Mom. You were awesome, Mom. You didn't have to be perfect. But you were just the perfect mother for me."

Skyla's heart sang with a gladness she hadn't felt since the day John died. "Thank you," she whispered, as she pulled away from Rowen and patted his cheek. A grown man's face.

She was not one of those mothers who still infantilized their adult children. Yet, she couldn't help but feel amazed at how her little boy had grown up to become such a kind and generous man, a father himself now, his heart so wide open it could now hold all the pain in this world and not crumble under all that weight.

She had been so terrified that Rowen would remember all the wrong things that she herself had forgotten all the wonderful memories of his childhood.

She knew what to do now. At their next family dinner, Skyla would bring out all of Rowen's childhood pictures and videos—and she had stocked up an almost endless supply—to regale her son and his family.

And to remind herself of the only truth that mattered, that no life was perfect but that she had ensured that the good times far outnumbered the bad ones.

"Thank you, Rowen," Skyla said, then wiped her tears and turned to walk the three blocks to her own apartment, the sun still generously spilling warm light on her head and the wind caressing her cheeks tenderly.

～

Ready for more fantasy short stories on the motherhood experience? Check out the collection, Your Mother's Nightmares: Six Troubling Tales, which includes five more twisted tales on the motherhood experience.

When you buy the collection directly from my store, please treat yourself to a 40% discount using the code YMN40.

Please note the code YMN40 is valid only for the short story collection — Your Mother's Nightmares: Six Troubling Tales — in ebook format when purchased directly from my PayHip store, Dream Pedlar Books.
Go to https://payhip.com/b/SfQvj to redeem your code!

ENJOYED MEMORY GAMES?

Thank you for reading *Memory Games*!

If you loved the story, I hope you will consider writing a short review—even a simple line or two—on the site where you bought the book.

Publishing is still driven by word of mouth, and when you leave a review it helps other readers decide this is a story worth reading. Thank you for your help in spreading the word.

You can also sign up to my monthly newsletter for updates on new book releases as well as heartfelt reflections on writing, reading, parenting and living the creative life.

Monthly Missives from The Dream Pedlar
https://thedreampedlar.com/newsletter

AUTHOR'S NOTE

Dear Reader,

Mommy guilt! Parental guilt! Gosh! So much of our parenting/motherhood journeys are marred by this feeling. It haunts us constantly.

Naturally, I wrote this story out of a desperate desire to remove every mistake I've made from the memory of my little child, D (Dhruv). It's as if something in me simply won't allow me to make mistakes when it comes to parenting, and will castigate me endlessly every time I slip up.

I had a lot to say on this topic of parental guilt—the usual sermons on how futile it is, how it only keeps us from accepting our essentially flawed and altogether human selves —but I think this article titled *Parent Guilt: A Silent Epidemic* by Robin Grille over at The Natural Child Project says it all really well.

https://www.naturalchild.org/articles/robin_grille/
parent_guilt.html

The TL;DR version is that ours is the first generation of parents looking to care for our children's mental and emotional wellbeing when our own needs in these areas were likely not met.

So we're quite literally learning by doing, we are complete beginners at this, and it is grace, not guilt, that will carry us through this very arduous task.

Like my friend Xue says, we all need 'study buddies' on this lifelong learning journey of parenting well!

Thank you for reading this far, dear Reader. I'd love to stay in touch with you. And I hope you'd like to stay connected with me too.

I send out a monthly newsletter on the last Sunday of every month filled with heartfelt musings on the joys of writing, reading and living the creative life. Subscription is free.

You will be the first to hear of my forthcoming works. I also include updates on my writing life, book recommendations, free short fiction, and occasional surprises.

Thank you for staying with me this far. If you choose to accompany me further on this journey, I promise you a magical ride.

Climb aboard at https://thedreampedlar.com/newsletter!

~ Anitha Krishnan
Burlington, Ontario
Tuesday, 18 June 2024

MORE BOOKS BY ANITHA KRISHNAN

https://thedreampedlar.com/books/

Dying Wishes

Finalist, 2023 Rakuten Kobo Emerging Writer Prize in Speculative Fiction

A contemporary fantasy novel weaving Hindu mythology and South Indian folklore into a quest for belonging across different worlds — the World of Mortals and the World of Gods, India and Canada, the past and the present, the world outside and the one within.

Erased from Existence

A paranormal mystery in which a fifteen-year-old is erased from the memories and perception of everyone. Trapped in oblivion, she will have to unearth and reveal long-buried family secrets to escape.

The Land of No Reflection

A fantasy tale of two sightless young women on the run from their homeland, having committed the unpardonable crime of seeing.

A Benevolent Goddess

A story of a goddess who is punished for her desire to help human beings but is unable to find salvation by any other means.

In Search of Leo

A fantasy tale exploring the gamut of emotions that loss and grief can stir.

The Mind Meddler

A short fantasy story on the games The Mind Meddler plays by sneaking thoughts into people's minds, until he meets the one person who can resist his unkind mischief.

Mrs. D'Souza's Dispute With God

A fantasy short story in which a school teacher, Mrs. D'Souza, dies unexpectedly and sets out in search of God to demand answers to her burning questions on life and death.

Hello, Dreamer! Poems & Dreams

An eclectic collection of 100 short poems encompassing musings on the universe and its mysteries, nature and human life, my secret longings and fears, love and heartbreak, the sun and the moon, the stars and the seas, light and shadow, and joy and nostalgia.

ABOUT THE AUTHOR

Anitha Krishnan is a speculative fiction author and an award-winning poet. Her fantasy novel, *Dying Wishes*, was a finalist for the 2023 Rakuten Kobo Emerging Writer Prize in the Speculative Fiction category.

She has lived in and left pieces of her heart in many places across the world including Singapore, Australia, Canada, and most of all in her beloved birthplace, India. She presently lives in Burlington, Ontario with her husband and their cherished child.

Find more books and her blog on the writing life at
https://thedreampedlar.com.

Sign up to her monthly newsletter at
https://thedreampedlar.com/newsletter
to receive heartfelt musings, exclusive updates, book
recommendations, free fiction, and more!